STORIES FROM BRAMBLY HEDGE

PRIMROSE
IN CHARG

Written by Alan MacDonald • Illustrated by Lizzie Sanders

Based on the world created by Jill Barklem

HarperCollins *Children's Books*

Jill Barklem created the world of Brambly Hedge in 1980 with the classic books *Spring Story*, *Summer Story*, *Autumn Story* and *Winter Story*, later followed by *The Secret Staircase*, *The High Hills*, *Sea Story* and *Poppy's Babies*. These enduringly popular books have sold more than 5 million copies, with the mice of Brambly Hedge appearing on merchandise and in their own animated television series.

Twenty-five years on, Brambly Hedge continues to delight both children and adults. The classics are now joined by new stories, recreating Jill Barklem's enchanting world for a new generation.

First published in paperback in Great Britain by HarperCollins Children's Books in 2007

1 3 5 7 9 10 8 6 4 2

ISBN-13: 978-0-00-783804-2

HarperCollins Children's Books is a division of HarperCollins Publishers Ltd.

Text and illustrations copyright © Jill Barklem 2007

Visit our website at: www.harpercollinschildrensbooks.co.uk

Printed and bound in Malaysia

Stories from Brambly Hedge

BRAMBLY HEDGE is on the other side of the stream, across the field, half-hidden under tangled roots and tall grasses.

This is the world of the little mice, Wilfred and Primrose, and their families.

The very best of friends, Wilfred and Primrose are always ready to share adventures.

Just like the time when they went to help Wilfred's granny look after three lively babies…

It was a fine spring day. Primrose and Wilfred were going to help Granny Toadflax look after Poppy's three babies.

Poppy's house had a lot of stairs. Granny stopped to catch her breath.

"Race you, Wilfred!" called Primrose. "Last one up is a crab apple!"

They found the babies, Pipkin, Rose and Buttercup, playing among piles of washing.

"Oh dear, I'm rather behind!" sighed Poppy.

"Never mind, you get on your way!" said Granny. "*I'll* take care of everything."

Poppy kissed each of the babies and set off,
promising to be back by tea time. She was going
to visit her cousin in Chestnut Woods.

Granny Toadflax settled in a rocking chair while
Primrose and Wilfred played with the babies on the floor.
"Peepo!" cried Wilfred, peeping between his paws.
Primrose had an idea. "Wouldn't Poppy be pleased if
we hung this washing out to dry?" she said.

They all trooped outside. Wilfred held the pegs
while Primrose hung the washing on the line.
The babies ran in and out of the
billowing sheets and clothes.
"Beepo!" they squealed excitedly. "Beepo!"

Back inside they found Granny Toadflax
had dozed off to sleep.

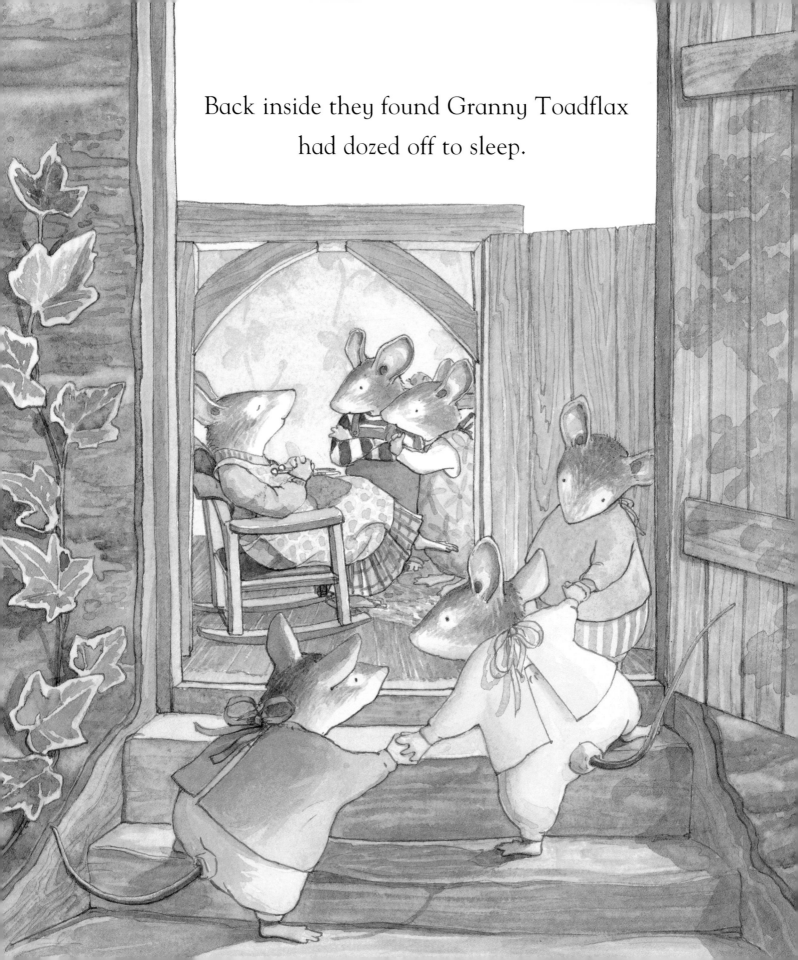

Primrose tiptoed past.
"Shh!" she whispered.

Wilfred looked around.
"Where did the babies
go?" he asked. "They
were here just now."

Pipkin, Rose and Buttercup were in the kitchen,
where they'd found a cake Poppy had made for tea.

"Oh no!" cried Primrose. "What a mess!"
The babies' paws and whiskers were
sticky with strawberry jam.

Primrose inspected what was left of the cake. "I'm sure I
can fix it," she said. "All it needs is some jam and icing."
"Couldn't we just eat it?" asked Wilfred hopefully.

They rummaged in the cupboards, looking for jam and
icing sugar. The babies crawled inside to help.
"Beepo! Beepo!" they called.

Wilfred spread jam
on the cake...

...while Primrose mixed
the icing in a bowl.

Pipkin, Rose and
Buttercup had found a
big bag of flour.

At last the cake was finished. "There!"
said Primrose proudly. "How does it look?"
"Sort of splodgy," said Wilfred. "But nice."

Wilfred looked under the table.
"Where did the babies go?"

There was no sign of them.

Wilfred pointed to a trail of tiny, sticky footprints crossing the kitchen floor. "Look! They went this way." The footprints led into the parlour where they circled round Granny Toadflax and, finally, disappeared.

Primrose looked worried. "Oh, Wilfred! We left the door open! What if they've run away?"

Outside they searched everywhere for the missing babies.

"Pipkin! Buttercup! Rose!" they called.
Muffled giggles came from somewhere close by.

Primrose pointed in dismay to the
washing line. "My sheets!" she cried.
"They've blown away!"
There was only one sheet left on the line.
Jammy paw prints stained the corners.
"Hmm," said Wilfred.
"I can guess who's been here."

They found one of
the sheets caught on
a hawthorn bush...

...and another one
dropped in a puddle.

They followed the trail to some tall grass that trembled and
shook. Out from behind it tottered a strange, white blob.
Wilfred clutched at Primrose, pretending to be scared.
"W... W... What is it?" he gasped.

Primrose pulled off the muddy sheet.
"BEEPO!" the babies giggled with delight.

Back in the house, Primrose and Wilfred filled the
bathtub with bubbles. The babies splashed and played
while Primrose soaked the dirty sheets in the basin.

They had almost got the
babies dressed, when they heard
the front door opening.
"Hello! I'm back!" called Poppy.

The babies climbed
downstairs excitedly.

Later, Poppy laid out a delicious tea with honey biscuits and a very sticky cake. "Mmm! This cake turned out even better than I expected," she smiled. "I do hope my little angels haven't been any trouble."

"Oh no," yawned Granny Toadflax, suddenly waking up. "They were no bother, no bother at all!"